For Crishell and Tasha
and remembering Lorraine

Encore, Grace!

MARY HOFFMAN

Cover illustration by Caroline Binch
Black and white illustrations by June Allan

F

FRANCES LINCOLN
CHILDREN'S BOOKS

Text copyright © Mary Hoffman 2003
Cover illustration copyright © Caroline Binch 2003

First published in Great Britain in 2003 by
Frances Lincoln Limited, 4 Torriano Mews
Torriano Avenue, London NW5 2RZ
www.franceslincoln.com

This edition first published in Great Britain in 2011

A catalogue record for this book is available from the British Library.

ISBN 978-1-84780-309-2

Printed in Croydon, Surrey, UK by CPI Bookmarque Ltd. in July 2011.

1 3 5 7 9 8 6 4 2

Contents

Grace is a girl who loves stories. There have been several about her so far: Amazing Grace, Grace and Family and all the stories in Starring Grace. And now here are eight more about the girl who lives with her ma and Nana and Paw-Paw the cat. The other members of her family are her papa, his wife Jatou and their children Bakary and Neneh, who live in The Gambia in west Africa.

In these new stories Grace discovers that her family is still changing and so is her group of friends. The gang who had so many adventures in Starring Grace face new situations. And as always, when things change for Grace, she turns to stories for inspiration...

Grace and the New Girl

"Guess what!" said Aimee. "We're getting a new girl in our class."

"Never!" said Grace, her imagination already working overtime.

For as long as she could remember, Grace's group of friends from school had been the same. Aimee was her best friend – they had known each other since kindergarten and their mums were friends too. Then there was Maria, who had joined their class in Year One and had so many brothers and sisters that she liked coming to play with Grace because she was an "only".

"Not that I'm really an only," thought Grace. "I have Neneh and Bakary." They were her half-sister and half-brother, but they lived in Africa with Grace's papa and his second wife Jatou. Grace didn't know them very well, but once a month she got a letter from

The Gambia and Neneh and Bakary put in a picture or a note for her. And every week her papa phoned her up and they had a talk about all their news.

Aimee and Maria were like sisters to Grace and she had two friends who were like brothers. They were Kester and Raj. They were both in her class at school. Kester was the biggest boy in the class, but he was gentle and kind too, though he didn't let everyone see it. And Raj didn't use to be Grace's friend at all until they were both in the play *Peter Pan*.

The "gang", as they called themselves, had become even closer over the summer when they were the ones who didn't go away on holidays. They all met in Grace's garden every day and made up adventures. Grace's nana helped them.

There were lots of other children in their school class, of course, and they were friends with some of them too. There was La Tasha, who was big and jolly and fun to be with. And there were George and Jason and Julio, who the boys played football with. The girls preferred netball.

There were other children they didn't get on so well with. Natalie, for example, who was a bit jealous of Grace's popularity, and Russell, who was a bully. But the five friends didn't have much to do with them.

"I wonder if the new girl will be a friend," said Grace, "or someone to steer clear of."

But Aimee didn't know anything about her, only that she was starting after half term. Her mum had heard it from Jason's mum, whose next-door neighbour was a first cousin of the new girl's dad.

In the first half of term, Grace's gang had spent a great two weeks being extras in the musical of *Annie* in a real theatre with lots of people. Then it was half term and the gang felt a bit flat. After all the excitement of being in a real show in a real theatre, they thought the rest of the term would be dull. The new girl was the only thing they had to look forward to.

"I hope she plays football," said Kester.

"I hope she hasn't already got a best friend," said Maria. She was very happy in Grace's gang but she had always wanted to be someone's best friend, the way Aimee was Grace's.

"We'll have the Christmas play this term too," said Grace quickly. "I wonder what it will be this time?"

But when they got back to school, there were two surprises on the first day.

The new girl was called Crishell. She was very pretty, with black curly hair, very long eyelashes and a beautiful smile. But she didn't show it often, because she wasn't at all friendly. In fact, she seemed a bit stuck-up.

Then, after she had introduced the new girl to them, their teacher, Ms Woollacott, said, "I've decided that this year the class Christmas play will be – *Sleeping Beauty!*"

A few girls squealed, but Grace's gang looked at one another in horror. There were only three decent parts in the story of *Sleeping Beauty* and two of them were what Kester called "wet".

"Bags I be Wicked Fairy," said Grace.

"Well, no one would cast you as Beauty," said Natalie, shaking her blond curls.

Grace didn't care, though she was glad when Aimee said, "How rude!" Grace didn't want to be someone who lay sleeping, waiting for a handsome prince to wake her up before her life could begin. She wanted to be someone who made things happen.

"Who do you think will be the prince?" whispered Maria.

"Kester," Raj whispered back, and that gave them all the giggles.

"Settle down," said Ms Woollacott. "And there's no need to roll your eyes, Kester. This is going to be no ordinary fairy tale. For a start, I want you to write your own version. We'll start with the gifts that the fairies give at the princess's christening. I want you all to make a list of the best things the baby could have. And the fairies can be boys or girls. Jason, please don't pull faces. You can make them superheroes if you want."

It was a most interesting class. They ended up with a list of christening guests and gifts that looked like this:

Glamour Fairy: Beauty (this came from Natalie and her group of special friends)

Superman: Superhuman strength (This was Kester's)

Fairy of friendship: Making friends (Maria's)

David Beckham: Football skills (from Jason and Julio and lots of the boys)

Madonna: Being able to sing and dance (Aimee's)

Cheerful Fairy: Happiness (La Tasha's)

Gold Fairy: Lots of money (from George and most of the class)

Tale Fairy: Being able to tell stories (Grace's)

Muse: Creativity (Crishell's)

"How many can we have?" asked Natalie.

"As many as we all agree on," said Ms Woollacott. "But remember, if Beauty has been given a special gift, she'll have to use it during the play. And don't forget we have to have the Bad Fairy and the Good Fairy too."

It was clear that this was going to be a much more interesting play than the children had first thought, with much more appealing parts. They were now competing to play Madonna and Becks and Superman and there was a lot of excited chatter.

Grace was unusually quiet. She kept looking at Crishell. The new girl had come up with an idea that Grace wished she had thought of and a word Grace didn't know. Crishell had explained to the class that a "muse" was a source of inspiration and that the ancient Greeks had nine of them, one for dancing, one for history, and so on.

"That's a wonderful idea, Crishell," Ms Woollacott had said. "I can see you're going to be a great asset to the class."

Grace was used to being the one in class who came up with that sort of idea. And although she had been in Ms Woollacott's class for only a few weeks, she was used to being the one whose ideas were praised. A horrible feeling was beginning to gnaw at her stomach.

By the time Nana came to meet her at the school gates, Grace was in a thoroughly bad mood. She scuffed her shoes through all the fallen leaves on her way home and didn't answer when Nana asked her how her day had been. But Nana knew Grace very well and she knew that the whole story would come out in her own good time. As they cut up carrots

together in the kitchen, Nana asked casually, "How was the new girl?"

"Awful," said Grace, savagely chopping her carrot. "I hate her."

"Really?" said Nana. "Is she so horrible, then? Is she rude to the teacher? Mean to the children? Unkind to the class rabbit?"

Grace's lips twitched. "No, none of that. But she's a show-off and she thinks she's too good for the rest of us."

"Ah," said Nana. "Maybe she's shy."

"No," said Grace. "She was full of ideas today and Ms Woollacott thinks she's the bee's knees."

Nana changed the subject then but later that evening, when Grace was supposed to be asleep, she heard Nana and Ma talking.

"I think Grace's nose has been put out of joint, Ava," Nana said. "This new girl is stealing her thunder."

Next morning, Grace looked hard at her nose in the mirror. Was it perhaps not quite as straight as it used to be?

She was not sure where she kept her thunder, but over the next few days she certainly felt her supply of it getting smaller, while Crishell's grew.

The play of Sleeping Beauty was now cast. After fierce competition, which didn't include Grace, Natalie was chosen to be the heroine. Her best friend Daisy was to be the Glamour Fairy. Kester was Superman and Raj was David Beckham. Maria was the Friendship Fairy. A girl called Bonnie was the Good Fairy and Grace was the Wicked one – though she wouldn't have minded being the Tale Fairy.

"No," said Ms Woollacott. "You were much the scariest Wicked Fairy, Grace." And she made Jason the Tale Fairy, though she agreed he could change his name to the Story Dude. Julio was the Prince and got teased a lot about having to kiss Natalie.

La Tasha was Madonna and Aimee was the Cheerful Fairy, even though they had suggested them the other way round. And Crishell was the Muse of Creativity. What with the king and queen and the herald and all the courtiers, everyone had a part.

"Now," said Ms Woollacott. "Who's going to write the play? You'll all have to contribute ideas, but we need one or two people to write them down and organise them into proper scenes."

Now Grace wanted to write the play more than she wanted a part. She raised her hand, thinking she would burst if Ms Woollacott didn't choose her. But what was this? No one else had their hand up except the new girl.

"Excellent," said Ms Woollacott, before Grace could change her mind and put her hand down. "Grace and Crishell will make excellent writers for us. Now, let's get to work."

Grace touched her nose. It definitely felt very crooked.

Grace and the
Green-Eyed Monster

—∞—

Grace couldn't believe she was going to be working with the new girl. Crishell was just as prickly on her own as she was in class. Every time Grace had an idea, Crishell had a different one. And the worst thing was that Crishell's were usually better.

"You have to keep trying," said Nana, when Grace complained about the new girl being so competitive. "Why don't you invite her back here one afternoon after school and you can work on the play together."

Grace wasn't at all sure she wanted Crishell in her home. "Perhaps she'll say no," Grace thought.

But Crishell was very polite and said yes, she'd love to come home with Grace the next afternoon after school.

"Won't you have to ask your mum?" said Grace.

"Oh no," said Crishell, as if she always did just what she liked. "She'll be fine."

Grace's gang all sat together at lunchtime. Crishell didn't have a regular place yet. Sometimes she sat with what the gang called "Natalie's cheerleaders", people like Daisy and Lynnette, and sometimes with Tasha. Today she stood hesitating with her lunch box and Raj said, "Look out – Her Majesty is coming over."

Raj didn't like Crishell because she had corrected his pronunciation during improvisation the first time they had tried the christening scene.

"I wish you loads of football skills," he said, "pacifically scoring goals."

"Don't you mean 'specifically', Raj?" Crishell had asked. "If you say 'pacifically', it means 'peacefully', and you can't really score a goal peacefully, can you?"

"Who does she think she is?" muttered Raj furiously to the rest of the gang. "She's not the teacher." But Ms Woollacott had agreed with Crishell. "Quite right, it's a common mistake," she said.

So now Raj pointedly turned round to talk to Kester when Crishell sat at their table. Conversation was very awkward. And it got worse when Russell came to join them too. Russell was definitely someone they steered clear of. He was quite a nice-looking boy, with clear grey eyes and a friendly smile. But he enjoyed hurting people and had once given Grace a painful Chinese burn. But he seemed really keen on Crishell. Soon he was talking only to her and Crishell was enjoying his attention.

"We should warn her, Grace," whispered Aimee. "You know how you can't tell what Russell's like by looking at him."

"I'm sure she can take care of herself," Grace whispered back.

The next day, Nana was waiting at the gates as usual to take Grace home. It was raining, so she had brought the car. Grace's heart sank as she saw Crishell flash her beautiful smile at Nana and heard her say "How do you do?" She thought that Nana wouldn't understand how she felt about this interloper.

Nana had baked lots of her best goodies

for the girls – peanut cookies and ginger buns and carrot cake. But Crishell would only nibble at a corner of one cookie. "No thank you," she said politely to everything else. "I have to be careful about my weight."

Grace and Nana exchanged stares. "Why, there's nothing of you!" said Nana. Then she left the two girls to their writing.

Once they were working on the play, things got a bit easier. Grace had never known anyone before who had as many ideas as her and, when it wasn't being annoying, it was quite exciting.

"We can't make it too long," said Crishell, "because all the other classes have to do their plays too. So we have to concentrate on the main scenes."

"Let's make a list," said Grace. "We start with the king and queen wanting a baby."

"Obviously," said Crishell. "But we'll keep it short, because Russell and Lynnette aren't the best actors."

"Then we could have someone with a placard saying 'NINE MONTHS LATER'," suggested Grace.

Crishell frowned. "It's a bit tacky, but OK. We haven't got time for changing seasons or anything."

"Then Lynette can give birth to the baby," said Grace. "We'll need a doll for that."

"And not too much moaning and groaning," said Crishell. "This is a fairy tale, not a soap opera."

"Right," said Grace, beginning to enjoy herself. "Then we need a scene with the king and queen writing christening invitations."

"And then the christening itself," said Crishell.

"Yes, that's the big one," said Grace, "with all the fairies and heroes and the Muse, of course."

Crishell helped herself casually to a ginger bun.

"And your big moment as the Wicked Fairy," she said.

By the time Crishell's mother came to pick her up, the girls had finished their list of scenes and written two of them.

"Can Grace come back to us tomorrow, Mummy?" asked Crishell.

Grace was very surprised, but both Nana and Crishell's mother said it would be OK.

"Again?" said Aimee, when Grace said she wouldn't be able to play after school because she had to work with Crishell. "She'll be your best friend soon at this rate."

"No way," said Grace. "But we've got to get the play finished."

Actually, Grace was looking forward to seeing where Crishell lived. But as soon as Crishell's mother drove up, Grace began to feel uncomfortable. The car was so shiny and new and had electric windows and a CD player and a heated windscreen. Nana's car was very old and had a broken fan so she had to wind down the driver's window to clear the condensation.

Crishell lived in a whole house with a garden of its own. Everything was tidy and super-clean. But although Crishell's mum was friendly, there was just one plate of shop-bought biscuits. And she said "Only one, honey," to Crishell, although Grace had eaten three by then.

"Would you like to see Crishell's room?" asked her mum, while Grace was awkwardly wiping crumbs off her mouth. Grace nodded, though Crishell looked embarrassed. The two girls went upstairs and Grace's jaw dropped when she saw Crishell's huge bed and dressing table and walk-in wardrobe.

"Wow!" she said, thinking of her own little room with its second-hand furniture. "You are lucky!"

Had she imagined it, or did Crishell brush away a tear?

"We'd better get on with the play," said Crishell. "There's lots more to write."

They got most of it finished that afternoon and by suppertime Grace was ravenous.

"You are the best cook in the world, Nana," she said, after her third helping of chicken and rice and peppers.

"What do you suppose that pretty child Crishell is having for her supper?" asked Nana.

"A stick of celery and three crispbreads, if she's lucky," said Grace, who didn't like it that Nana thought Crishell pretty. "I reckon her mum starves her."

"What's her house like?" asked Ma.

"Well, it's big and very clean and tidy," said Grace. "But there are no books, except

in Crishell's room, and that looks like something from Barbie's dream home".

"Well now," said Nana. "Am I hearing your opinion, Grace, or is that the green-eyed monster talking?"

"Who's the green-eyed monster?" asked Grace.

"Nana means 'jealousy'," said Ma, frowning. "But you aren't jealous of Crishell, are you, Grace?"

Grace didn't answer. She certainly hadn't felt like her old self ever since Crishell came on the scene and, although she thought it sounded lovely to have green eyes, she didn't want to be a monster to get them. She would have given anything for things to go back the way they were before half term.

Ms Woollacott was very pleased with all the girls' hard work and gave them both a merit point. "Now we can really get going with our rehearsals," she said.

They had called the play *Waking Beauty* because their version had far more action than usual after the kissing scene, and it looked as if it would be really good. As usual, Nana was roped in to help with the costumes. Grace and Crishell didn't need to work together any more but they somehow drifted into the habit of sitting near each other and Crishell joined the gang's lunch table several times more.

There never seemed to be much in her lunch box and she sometimes cast wistful looks at the hearty lunches which Nana packed for Grace. After a while, Grace took to bringing extra so that she had plenty to offer Crishell. And sometimes Crishell accepted. She always looked a bit furtive about it, glancing quickly round before sinking her perfect white teeth into a chicken drumstick or a spicy bun.

"I reckon she's anorexic," said Kester, who was always willing to eat Grace's extra food on top of his school lunch, on the days when Crishell didn't sit with them.

"Just because she's not as greedy as you!" said Aimee. "You might share that bun!"

After school that day, Grace went over the garden fence to visit her friend Mrs Myerson. The old lady lived in a house whose garden backed on to Grace's and the gang had made friends with her the summer before.

Today Grace had brought Mrs Myerson some of Nana's chicken soup in a thermos, as the old lady hadn't been very well. Grace could have perfectly well walked round the block to Mrs Myerson's, but she preferred the back garden route; it made it more of an adventure and she felt like Little Red Riding Hood going to visit her grandmother.

Mrs Myerson was more like her great-great-grandmother; she was very old and wrinkled. She came shuffling to the door, wrapped in a thick shawl, and smiled when she saw Grace.

"Ah, *liebchen*," she said, in her thick German accent. "Have you brought me something from your grandmother? She is so good to me."

Grace laid a place for Mrs Myerson and poured the soup for her. The old lady coughed a lot.

"Too much pepper?" asked Grace sympathetically.

"No, dear," said Mrs Myerson. "It's these silly old lungs of mine."

She couldn't finish the soup, but she sat in her armchair and asked Grace to tell her what she had been doing at school. Grace told her about the new girl and what Nana had said about the green-eyed monster. Soon she was telling Mrs Myerson all about Crishell's elegant mother and her pretty clothes and her Barbie bedroom and her flash car.

"But you say this child does not seem happy," said Mrs Myerson.

"No," said Grace. "She's not happy. Sometimes she has a little cry when she thinks no one is looking, and she has problems about eating."

"Are you happy, Grace?" asked Mrs Myerson, fixing her with her glittering eyes.

"Mm, yes – most of the time," said Grace.

"And you don't have any problems with eating, do you?" said Mrs Myerson, laughing her rusty old laugh, knowing how hungry the gang always was whenever she baked for them.

"None at all," said Grace, joining in. She remembered how Kester thought Mrs Myerson was like the witch in the gingerbread house the first time she offered them cakes.

"No," said Mrs Myerson. "You have a lovely mother and grandmother and your dear papa in Africa and you have lots of friends and a healthy appetite. It seems to me, Grace, that if anyone is having a visit from the green-eyed monster, it might be the other girl, not you."

Grace was very thoughtful when she left Mrs Myerson's house, after making her a cup of tea and a hot water bottle. She made up her mind to get to know Crishell properly.

Grace and the Toad

"Oh, no, my dear, we don't want to invite Malicia Badheart," said Russell, adjusting his cardboard crown. "We haven't got enough fancy gold plates to go round."

"All right then, if you're sure she won't mind," said Lynnette, trying not to trip over her dress, which had once been a nightie of her mother's. She was rather enjoying being queen to Russell's king, since Natalie and all her friends were rather keen on him.

There were only two weeks left to go before the play and most of the children had learned their parts. They were trying out bits of costumes already, so that they could get used to them. The next scene had more people than any other and soon the hall stage was filled with fairies and courtiers and heroes.

Raj wore his football gear and La Tasha looked fantastic as Madonna in a leather skirt and lacy black gloves. Kester wore his Superman T-shirt, which everyone had seen before, but this time Nana had made him a bright red cloak to go with it.

Crishell was wearing a cloak too, a long silvery one over a silver leotard.

"You look great," said Maria.

"How do you know the Muse wears a silver leotard?" asked Natalie.

"How do you know she doesn't?" said Crishell.

Grace had thought about her costume for a long time. She had found an old pair of woolly gloves that Ma said she could cut the fingers off. She borrowed Mrs Myerson's second-best walking stick and was wrapped in an old lace curtain which Nana had dyed black. On the day of the performance, she was going to paint her finger-nails black and wear an old witch's hat left over from Halloween.

Now she burst on to the stage, just after the Muse had bestowed her gift of creativity on the baby – which was a Tiny Tears doll currently being clutched upside down by Lynnette.

"Ha-ha!" Grace cackled. "Someone seems

to be having a party and *someone* seems to have forgotten my invitation!"

After the rehearsal, Grace bumped into Crishell in the props cupboard. Again she noticed a small tear, but this time Grace decided to do something about it.

"Has someone been mean to you?" she demanded, still looking menacing in her fingerless gloves. "Is it Russell?"

Crishell dashed the tear away with the back of her hand. "No," she said, surprised. "Why Russell?"

"Because he's a bully," said Grace.

Crishell sighed. "It's nothing as simple as being bullied," she said.

And then it all came out. How unhappy she was, how her dad had left them and her mum kept trying to make it up to her by buying things. How, because her dad had gone off with a younger, thinner, woman, Crishell's mum had become obsessed with dieting and being slim. How Crishell was always hungry but didn't like to ask for more food in case it upset her mother, and how she was afraid to buy more food even though she had plenty of pocket money, because she didn't want to put on any weight in case her mother stopped loving her. And how miserable she was in a new school where she didn't have any friends and missed her old ones. And how that made her snippy so that she couldn't make any new ones.

Grace just sat on the floor with her mouth open while all Crishell's unhappiness came flooding out. When she had cried herself to a stop, Crishell mopped her eyes and said, "I would give anything to be you, Grace. You're so sure of yourself and so popular."

So Mrs Myerson had been right! Crishell was more jealous of Grace than the other way round. It made Grace feel giddy to think how little she had understood.

"Sure of myself? You must be kidding!" said Grace. "You know my ma and papa broke up too. I was very small. I don't really remember him from then. But when I went to visit him and his new wife in Africa, I was a mess! I was horrible to Jatou, even though she's a really nice person and I like her now. And my ma's got a boyfriend and I don't want her to marry him, but I think she might. And we don't have much money, not nearly as much as your family and my ma's always worrying about it."

But Grace didn't want to pretend to be unhappy when she wasn't, not really. "I think everyone's got problems, if you ask them," she said. "But one thing I reckon is *really* bad is your mum not giving you enough food. Let's see what I've got left in my lunch-box."

Crishell was still sniffing and saying she didn't want anything, but Grace made her eat the rather squashed chocolate bar she had saved to have on the way home.

"You need it for shock," she said. "It's like a shock when you tell someone else all your problems. But I'm glad you did."

"So am I," said Crishell, licking the chocolate off her fingers.

And from then on, Grace and Crishell were proper friends.

One of the first things Grace did was tell the gang that Crishell wasn't stuck-up at all, just very unhappy. She didn't give away any of the new girl's secrets; she just wanted to make them be nicer to her. Raj wasn't convinced, but he agreed to try.

Crishell now sat with them most lunchtimes. The problem was that Russell often came and sat with them too. He seemed really keen on Crishell but she was a bit wary of him since Grace had told her about his bullying.

There was another problem too, though Grace didn't spot it straight away. It was Aimee. She had become very quiet, not speaking to Crishell and hardly saying anything to Grace or the rest of the gang.

"Have you noticed anything wrong with Aimee?" asked Maria one morning, when she got Grace on her own. "She doesn't seem like her old self at all. I don't know how she's going to be the Cheerful Fairy."

Grace felt guilty. She had been so full of her own concerns, worrying about Ma and Vincent and about Mrs Myerson's cough and about how to solve Crishell's eating problem, and perfecting her part in the play, that she hadn't noticed anything wrong with Aimee.

Now, during rehearsal, she was especially friendly to Aimee, praising her for her performance, even though privately she agreed with Maria that Aimee was proving a very doleful giver of happiness.

"You look nice in your costume, Aimee," she said. "Like Minnie Mouse." Aimee was wearing a red and white polka dot skirt with a matching bow in her hair.

Aimee managed a smile. "And you look totally evil in yours," she said.

"Thanks!" said Grace. Then, "Is anything the matter, Aimee? You've been a bit down lately."

Aimee gave a big sigh. "It's nothing."

But Grace persisted and eventually Aimee said, in a very small voice, "I thought you might want to best friends with Crishell now, instead of me."

Grace was amazed. "Don't be silly! She's only been here a few weeks. and I've known you for ever."

"But she's much prettier than me," said Aimee, "and she's cleverer too, more like you."

Grace didn't know what to say. She didn't think about either Aimee or Crishell in that way. And yet it was interesting having someone new in the class. And she did find

Crishell exciting to be with, because she was always so full of ideas.

So she just gave Aimee a big hug and told her she was sorry for neglecting her. "Let's have a sleepover at my place this weekend," she said. "Just you, me and Maria."

Now that she had sorted out things out with Aimee, Grace began to notice what was going on with Maria. During rehearsals, Russell had started picking on her.

It was true that Maria wasn't one of the best actors in the class; she was too shy in front of people she didn't know well. And if she got something wrong, she tended to go to pieces. She had only a few lines, in the christening scene, but Grace and Crishell had made them good ones:

I am the Fairy Pal who sends
The gift of making lots of friends.
When I wave my magic wand around
The princess will be the most popular babe
in town.

"She's not waving it at all," complained Russell loudly. "Besides, how can she be the Fairy Pal? She doesn't look as if she's got any friends."

"Shut up, Russell," said Kester, flexing his muscles under his Superman shirt. "Maria's got lots of friends – and I'm one of them."

Russell behaved himself for the rest of the rehearsal but when the gang weren't nearby, he took to taunting Maria.

"They're not really your friends. Grace has Aimee and Kester has Raj. You're just a spare wheel."

Russell was like that. Sometimes he hit little kids or did something else to hurt them but usually he got his kicks from making people unhappy, especially girls. He liked to see them cry.

But Crishell saw what was happening and told Grace, and together they hatched a plot. Because the class was performing *Waking Beauty*, they were reading all sorts of traditional tales and could choose which ones they liked best. Sometimes they rewrote them to bring them up to date.

Grace and Crishell chose one called 'Diamonds and Toads' and Ms Woollacott asked them to read it out in class. This is how it went:

Once upon a time there was a sweet, good-natured girl who had a stepbrother who was always mean to her. One day her stepmother sent her to a well to fetch a bucket of water. And when the girl got there, she found a tiny old woman who asked her for water. "Of course," said the girl, and gave the woman a drink. When the girl got back home and her mean stepbrother started teasing her, she opened her mouth to tell him to stop – and out fell a diamond.

The stepbrother called his mother and they asked the girl to explain what had happened to her but with every word she said, more jewels, and flowers too, fell out of her mouth. Soon the floor was covered with diamonds and emeralds and roses and lilies.

"We're rich!" said the stepmother. "Son, you must go and fetch water from the well too, so we can be even richer."

So the mean stepbrother set out, grumbling

all the way, and reached the same well. "Will you give me some water?" asked the old woman, who was still there.

"No, why should I? Get your own," said the boy rudely. And he took his bucket of water back home.

"There's my lovely boy," said his mother. "Speak to me, son!"

"Don't be so soft," said the rude boy, pushing his mother away.

And a great toad fell out of his mouth.

"Yeugh!" screamed his mother. "What happened?" But as the boy tried to tell her, a snake slithered out of his mouth, followed by a scorpion and a rat.

The girl left home and married a handsome prince and was always rich because of the jewels that fell from her lips, and always had fresh flowers in her room. But the boy and his mother lived unhappily ever after, and it served them right.

Everyone clapped.

"Very good," said Ms Woollacott. "But why did you turn the stepsister into a stepbrother?"

Most of the class looked at Russell.

"Because boys can be mean as well,"

said Grace. "And when they say spiteful things, it's like horrible creepy-crawlies coming out of their mouths."

Maria didn't have any trouble with Russell after that. If ever he started picking on her, one of gang would just say, "I see a toad!" and he would stop.

Grace and the Changes

The next time Grace went to visit Mrs Myerson after school, the old lady was impressed by her account of how she had handled Russell.

"Quite right," said Mrs Myerson. "You should never let the bullies get away with it. I'm proud of you, Grace, because I know it's not easy to stand up to them."

"You were right about Crishell, too," said Grace. "She was a bit jealous of me, but we're good friends now."

"I'm glad," said Mrs Myerson, suppressing a cough. "You can't have too many friends. Look how much good it's done me, having you and your gang as friends. Before you came into my garden last summer, I used to look at children from behind my bars and I was always afraid that they would trample on my flowers or break my windows."

Grace gave her a hug. "So you didn't grow flowers any more – at least, not until we came along."

Mrs Myerson laughed her rusty creaking laugh until she had another bad coughing fit. When she had recovered, she said, "Ah, the flowers of last summer! I wonder if I shall see them again?"

⸺⸺

The first cold days of winter had come and Grace was feeling strange. Now, when she got up in the morning it was only just getting light and by the time she got home from school it was getting dark again. It made Grace grumpy.

"Why do we have to have winter?" she grumbled to Nana. "What's the point of it? No one can go out to play except at weekends. Paw-paw spends all day snoozing by the radiator and I have to bundle up in all these woolly clothes. I wish I was with Papa in Africa where it's always hot."

Nana smiled. Nothing ever seemed to make her grumpy. "Why, honey," she said. "You are in a bad mood. What about all your favourite winter things – like buttered muffins and hot chocolate with marshmallows when you get in from school and sledging in the snow and Christmas?"

Grace licked the chocolate moustache off her top lip and managed a smile. "I do like hot food when it's cold outside," she admitted. "But it's nowhere near cold enough for snow and Christmas is ages away."

"Maybe," said Nana, "what you don't like is change. You like summer things and winter things but you don't like getting from one to the other."

"That's right," said Grace, brightening. "Though I don't mind changing from winter to summer, I think. I can't remember."

"You haven't done it as many times as I have," said Nana. "When you get to be old like me, the seasons seem to come around quicker and quicker, flick, flick, like your flicker book. No sooner have I got settled into my winter ways then along comes summer again."

"Perhaps that's what autumn and spring are for," said Grace. "To get us used to the changes."

"You're right," said Nana. "And you know what? Your papa in Africa always says he wishes their seasons changed a bit more slowly. It's hot sun for most of the year there and then one day suddenly, *sploosh*, it's the rainy season and everyone stays in or gets wet for weeks on end."

Grace often thought back to what Nana had said during the next few weeks, when there were far more changes to come than just weather.

The first thing happened the very next weekend. The whole gang were at Grace's. They were all wrapped up warm against the wind and were sitting at the outside table trying to decide what to do. Grace sat in the tyre that hung from the big old horse-chestnut tree, swinging her legs.

"We could be arctic explorers," she suggested, "and find the North Pole."

"You need snow for that," objected Kester, "and there's been hardly any this year."

"Yes," said Maria. "Let's wait till the snow comes for finding the Pole."

"Pity," said Raj. "I think I can see it." He was shading his eyes and looking at one end of the washing line.

"It's not exploring if you can see what you

are looking for," said Grace. "They're right. We'll wait till it's snowing again. What do you think, Aimee?"

To everyone's horror, Aimee burst into tears. Grace jumped out of the swing and rushed over and everyone else patted Aimee on the shoulder.

"I might not be here when the snow comes again," she sobbed. "You'll have to find the Pole without me."

"But why?" asked Grace. "Why won't you be here? Are you going on holiday?"

Aimee shook her head. "It's much worse than that. We're moving away. My dad's got a new job."

Everyone was shocked. Aimee and her family had lived in the next street to Grace's for as long as they could remember.

"Do you mean the other side of town?" asked Maria.

"No," said Aimee miserably. "The other side of the country."

"You can't do that!" said Grace. "You'd have to go to a different school. I'm going to ask Ma if you can live with us."

That cheered Aimee up and they spent the rest of the morning pretending to rescue her from prison. Aimee was very glad to be rescued, because she didn't like the spiders in prison, which was Grace's garden shed.

But when they went in to eat their packed lunch at the kitchen table, it suddenly didn't seem so easy for Grace to rescue Aimee from moving away.

"I hear your dad has a new job, Aimee," said Nana, as she made them all a hot drink.

Aimee, who had almost forgotten, looked sad again. "It's a long way away," she said.

"Yes and so much for your ma to do," said Nana, "finding a new place to live so near Christmas."

"That takes ages, doesn't it?" asked Grace.

"I shouldn't think you'll be able to move for months," said Kester. "It took that long when we moved, and that was in the same town!"

"Not months," said Nana. "Your ma said you'd move into somewhere rented first. She wants you all to be there for Christmas, so your dad can start his new job with the New Year."

When Grace's mother got in from work, she

saw straight away that she was going to be asked something important. Grace's eyes were big and solemn and she didn't say anything until Ma had drunk her two cups of tea and kicked her shoes off.

Then she told her about Aimee.

"That's too bad," said Ma. "You girls have known each other since you were tiny. And I'll miss Carol too."

"But can't we do something?" begged Grace. "We can't just let them go."

"What can we do?" asked Ma. "Good jobs are hard to come by and they wouldn't be going unless it was a better job for Joe."

"It is," said Nana. "It's a lot more money."

"But couldn't Aimee live with us?" asked Grace. "She could share my room and she doen't eat much."

Ma started to smile but then she saw that Grace was serious. So she pulled her up on to the sofa beside her and put her arm round her. "You know we can't do that," she said. "Aimee wouldn't want to live away from her own mother and father and her brother. Not really, not when it came to actually doing it.

You wouldn't like not to live with me and Nana, would you?"

"The very idea!" said Nana, and Grace knew that Ma was right.

The next afternoon, when the gang assembled at Grace's, they were all in a grumpy mood.

"It's not fair," said Raj. "We have to do whatever grown-ups decide."

"They never ask us what we want," said Maria. "My mum was talking to my nan the other day about sending me to a different school and she never even asked what I thought."

"That's it!" said Grace. "We have no rights! I'm going to do something about it."

"What?" asked Aimee, who was red-eyed from crying all night.

"We'll draw up a list of children's rights – a sort of charter – and then we can get grown-ups to sign it."

"What grown-ups?" asked Kester.

"Well, our parents, for a start," said Grace. "And maybe teachers, too, when we go back to school."

"What will it say?" asked Aimee.

"I don't know yet," said Grace. "Let's get some paper and write down our ideas. It's too wet to play outside anyway."

So the children sat up at the kitchen table with pens and scrap paper, just as if they were at school.

"Isn't this supposed to be a day of rest?" asked Nana. "You all look very busy. Still, as long as you have something to occupy you. I'm just popping over to see Gerda Myerson. She still isn't very well, I'm afraid. I'll be back soon."

So Nana went off to visit their old neighbour and the children drew up their charter, each of them choosing a clause especially close to their hearts:

CHILDREN'S RIGHTS

* Parents are not to move house without consulting us (Aimee's clause)
* Parents are not to decide which school children are to go to without talking to children first (Maria's)

* Children should have some say about what's going to be for dinner (Kester's)
* Children should be allowed to choose their own clothes, even when they are presents (Raj's)
* Parents shouldn't be allowed to get divorced or re-married without asking their children first (Grace's)
* Grown-ups should tell children what's going on (everyone's)

"They'll never agree to it," said Kester, gloomily. "Grown-ups just do what they want."

"But we have to try," said Grace, so they wrote out five copies in their neatest handwriting.

"Your Nana's been gone a long time," said Maria.

They had been so busy with the charter that they hadn't noticed. But at that moment Nana came in, looking very worried.

"I'm sorry it took so long," she said. "I'm afraid Gerda is much worse than I realised. I had to call an ambulance and wait for it to come. She's gone to the hospital."

"Oh poor Mrs Myerson!" said Grace.

"Can we go and see her?" asked Kester.

"I think it will be a while before she's up to visitors," said Nana.

"We could make her some get-well cards," said Aimee.

And all five of them did. They liked Mrs Myerson. She had bars on all her windows and strong locks on every door because she was frightened of people, but she liked the children. They had met her last summer when they thought that her house was haunted and that she was a witch. Ever since then they had looked after her garden and done chores for her, and she had made them delicious cakes and biscuits and told them stories.

That evening, when Ma came home, Grace showed her the cards.

"Well, I think that Mrs Myerson will love having these," Ma said. "I'll take them to her before work tomorrow and put them on her locker where she can see them."

"Did you see her today?" asked Grace, because she knew that it would have been her mother who found a bed for Mrs Myerson at the hospital.

"Yes, I recognised her name on the admissions sheet and I went up to the ward to visit her before I came home," said Ma.

"How was she?" asked Nana.

Ma looked serious. "She's very poorly," she said. "She has pneumonia and she's very frail."

"But she will be all right, won't she?" asked Grace, suddenly feeling very tight and scared in her tummy.

"I don't know," said Ma gently. "She's a very old lady, Grace – nearly ninety – and she has had a very hard life."

Grace put her hands over her ears. She didn't want to hear about it.

"What did you do with your friends today?" asked Ma, to change the subject.

Grace showed her the charter, because all the gang had promised to show their parents.

"Hm," said Ma. "Is this about Aimee, or about me and Vincent?"

Vincent was Ma's boyfriend and Grace had been worried, when she first started seeing him in the summer, that they might get married. She had spied on them until the night Ma told her that she hadn't thought about it yet.

But Grace still worried. She didn't like changes.

"I've already made the dinner, Grace," said Nana. "But you can choose what we eat tomorrow."

"I don't mind," said Grace, giving Nana a big hug. "All your dinners are lovely. That one was Kester's."

That night, when Ma was putting her to bed, Grace clung on to her extra hard.

"Ma," she said. "I don't like it that Nana is getting old."

"But Nana is fine, Grace," said Ma. "She isn't nearly as old as Mrs Myerson, you know, and she is pretty healthy."

"Nana says I don't like changes," said Grace, "and it's true. Why do things have to change?"

"That's a hard one," said Ma. "But not all changes are bad. What about the change you made in Mrs Myerson's life? Before she met all you children, she was a sad and frightened person. Whatever happens to her now, she's happy again in her old age – because of you."

That made Grace feel better.

"And I promise," said Ma, "that I will try to

talk to you more and tell you more about what's going on in my life, so you don't get any unwelcome surprises, just as you wanted in your charter. OK?"

"OK," said Grace. But as she settled down to sleep, she thought that there are some things that happen which can't be covered by any charter.

Grace says Goodbye

Next day, after school, the gang got together to talk about showing the charter to their parents. Aimee was much more cheerful. Her parents hadn't changed their minds about moving but they agreed they should have told her about her dad applying for the new job.

"They said they only didn't tell me because they didn't think he'd get it," she said. "And Mum says I can come and visit Grace in the Easter holidays, if that's OK."

"I'm sure it will be," said Grace. "And we can write to one another and talk on the phone. My ma says she'll tell me more about things too." What Grace didn't say was that she thought all the things would be about Vincent.

"My mum says she didn't know I don't like mince," said Kester with a big grin. "So now we don't have to have it. Except in spaghetti bolognese, and I love that."

"My parents say I don't have to go to a new school until we change over to the big one," said Maria.

"And mine say that I don't have to wear the sweater auntie Shamila knitted me for my birthday," said Raj. "I have to be nice about it, so as not to hurt her feelings, but they'll tell her what I'd like for Christmas."

"So it worked!" said Grace. "We should think of some more rules for grown-ups."

But just then the phone rang and Nana answered it. When she came off, she looked very serious.

"Something has happened," she said. "That was Grace's ma ringing from the hospital. I'm very sorry to say that Gerda Myerson has just died."

The children were too shocked to say anything. For all of them, it was the first time that someone they knew had died.

Nana bustled round making hot chocolate for all of them, but Grace saw her flick away some tears from her eyes. She gave Nana a big hug. Then she remembered something.

"What about poor Yowler?" she said. "Who's been feeding him?"

"I have," said Nana. "Leastways, I did last night and this morning. But I suppose we should bring him over here."

"Paw-paw won't like that," said Maria.

Paw-paw had been there in the garden the first time they had met Jauler, the Siamese cat. Jauler had blue eyes and a long thin chocolate and cream body. He had an unearthly yowl, which was what had made the children think the house was haunted. And it was what gave him his name, which sounded like "Yowler" if you said it in the German way. So that was how the children thought of him.

"Paw-paw will just have to put up with it," said Nana firmly, "until we decide what else to do."

She sat down suddenly. "There is so much to do. A whole house full of things to sort out – the cat is the least of it."

"Isn't there anyone to do all that?" asked Kester.

"No," said Nana. "She lost all her family in the war. An uncle brought her to England and left her that house when he died. He had no other family himself. I think we're the ones who'll have to make all the arrangements."

"Shall we go and get Yowler now?" asked Grace.

They all decided it was a good idea. So as soon as they'd finished their drinks, they fetched Paw-paw's basket and went round to Mrs Myerson's house. Nana had the keys and it took a long time to open the door. All was still and quiet in the house, as if it was waiting. Then came the high shriek which had so scared the children last summer.

Now they all called to the cat and Aimee picked Yowler up and stroked him. The cat struggled to get down, but that was nothing to the fuss he made about being put in the basket. All of a sudden he seemed to have about sixteen legs and to be made entirely of claws and teeth. It took all five children and Nana to get him safely fastened in and he yowled all the way back to Grace's flat.

"Poor Yowler," said Grace. "He doesn't like changes either."

They spent the rest of the day coaxing the Siamese cat with milk and titbits. The cat-flap had to be screwed up or Yowler would have raced over the gardens back to his own house. Paw-paw didn't think much of that. And he didn't think much of having Yowler to stay either. Meeting him in the garden was one thing, but sharing his home with him was quite another. In the end, Paw-paw went and stood by the back door until Grace took the hint and let him out.

Shortly afterwards, Yowler sank into an exhausted heap on Aimee's lap. He was still there when her mother came to pick her up. Aimee's mother, Carol, stayed for a cup of tea with Nana to talk about Mrs Myerson.

"Did she not even see the cards the children made?" Carol asked in a whisper, but Grace heard her. And she also heard Nana answer, "I never thought to ask. I'll ask Ava as soon as she gets in."

"Aimee looks happy with that cat on her lap though, doesn't she?" said Carol. "She's been so miserable since we told her about the move. I thought she would be terribly upset about Gerda."

"They all are," said Nana. "But animals can be a comfort. You know, that cat's going to need a new home and I don't think Paw-paw will want it to be ours."

Aimee's mother looked thoughtful.

———⚬⚬⚬———

Because Mrs Myerson was Jewish, the funeral was going to happen very quickly. All the children were going. The boys' parents weren't been too sure about it, but Kester and Raj both insisted. "She hasn't anyone else to be there," said Kester. "We're her family really," said Raj. So they all had the day off from school.

Grace's ma told them that Mrs Myerson had read all their cards and was happy to have seen them.

"She died very peacefully," said Ma. "She fell asleep and just drifted away."

The children wanted to do something else for their old friend but they didn't know what. They went to the flower shop but everything was so expensive. "It's because it's winter," said the assistant, sympathetically. "Can't you find anything in your gardens?"

But only Grace had a garden and there wasn't much growing there at present.

"I know," said Maria. "Let's see what we can

find in Mrs Myerson's own garden."

The children were very used to climbing the fence into the old lady's back garden but Nana said they could walk round with her and she'd let them through. She still had a lot of tidying up to do in the house.

"There are no flowers here either," said Maria, disappointed.

"But look," said Grace, "there are berries – lots of them!"

So the children cut down branches of holly and firethorn and cotoneaster and made a huge bunch. They wove ivy leaves in among the red berries and came back sucking their fingers from the holly prickles. Nana found a big red ribbon in her workbox that had been round Grace's last Easter egg, and they tied it round the stems of the branches.

"I think that will look just fine," said Nana, "and you can make one last card that says who it's from."

On the morning of the funeral the children put on their best clothes. "Make them nice and colourful," Nana had said. "Gerda had enough sadness in her life."

So the little party stood out brightly in the synagogue, even though the girls had to sit separately upstairs. There were a few old people from the neighbourhood who had known Mrs Myerson and some of them gave the children disapproving looks. But they all admired the sheaf of scarlet and crimson berries that lay at the feet of the cloth-wrapped body. The sight of the small canvas bundle that was all that was left of their friend, made the children very solemn.

Ma and Nana invited everyone back to their flat for a cup of tea and some of Nana's best cakes after the service. And the old people saw how polite the children were and heard them talk sadly about their friend.

"You must be the children who gave Gerda back her garden," said one old lady. "Do you know, before she met you, she wouldn't come to synagogue on her own. She'd only come if someone could give her a lift. But in the last few months, she often walked there and never missed a service. That was because of you."

It made the children feel better. "A good deed lasts for ever," said Nana.

"What about a bad one?" asked Grace, who remembered they had lied to Nana the first time they met Mrs Myerson.

"Oh a bad one can be made better by saying sorry or doing a good one," said Nana. "But you can never make a good deed bad."

"I was thinking," said Aimee's mother. "Perhaps it would be a good deed for someone to give that cat a new home."

Yowler was sitting on the windowsill trying to out-stare Paw-paw, who was on the back of the sofa, lashing his tail.

"Do you mean us?" said Aimee, who couldn't believe her luck.

"Well," said Carol. "If he stays here, he's going to keep running back to his old home. You can't keep him indoors for ever. And he'll miss his owner far more here than he would in a new place. It's time for him to move on."

"That's a very kind offer," said Ma. "What do you think, Grace?"

"It would be a good deed for Yowler," said Grace slowly, "and for Paw-paw too."

"And for Mrs Myerson," said Maria. "She'd

be glad to know he has a new home and isn't sad for her."

So it was agreed. And three days later, Aimee came with a new cat basket. She had been making a great fuss of Yowler ever since they collected him from Mrs Myerson's and he was much easier to get in the basket this time.

Aimee's parents and her little brother were waiting for her in the car outside. A big removal lorry had taken all their furniture to put into store and they just had a little trailer with their luggage to help them get by in their rented flat, until they bought their new home.

All the children were there to say goodbye to their friend. They said goodbye to Yowler too, who made such a loud noise when he was put in the car that it made it easier to part from Aimee.

She hugged them all and saved the last hug for Grace.

"I'll be back soon," she said.

"I know," said Grace. "Write and tell me how Yowler gets on."

And then they were gone.

The children went back into Grace's flat.

"We're not the Famous Five any more," said Kester.

"We never were," said Maria.

"But now we're the *Four* No One Has Heard Of," said Raj.

"We don't have to be," said Grace.

"What do you mean?" asked Maria. "Have you thought of a way for us to be famous?"

"No," said Grace. "I've thought of a way not to be four. We'll get a new person to join the gang."

Everyone spoke at once.

"Who?"

"Not Natalie."

"That's not fair to Aimee."

"I don't know," said Grace. "Not Natalie, I agree. But we'll find someone. And it's not unfair to Aimee. She'll make new friends where she's going. It's part of moving on. And we should do the same."

Grace on Thin Ice

It was very strange going back to school without Aimee. And of course someone else had to play the Cheerful Fairy in the class play. Ms Woollacott chose a girl called Lucy-Wei, who had previously been a court lady. There was only a week to go before the performance.

"It won't be the same without Aimee," wailed Maria.

"Do stop saying that!" said Grace. "Of course it won't be the same. How could it be? If it was the same, it would mean that Aimee didn't matter."

"Yeah," said Kester. It's like with Mrs Myerson. She and Yowler aren't there any more and it's no good pretending we can go and visit them, because we can't." He folded his arms and looked fierce. Crishell came over and gave him a hug and Kester's face turned bright pink. But he didn't push her away.

Crishell was spending more and more time with Grace's gang now. She was the only one who seemed to understand why they were so sad about the old lady's death. Natalie had said, "I don't see why you got a day off – it's not as if she was a relative."

But Crishell said, "You can be closer to some friends than you are to some relatives."

Now everyone in the group brought extra food in case Crishell was hungry, and she was starting to look less skinny. Even Raj was beginning to accept her as a friend. "But I'll never like her as much as Aimee," he warned Grace privately.

Now it was Crishell who came up with an idea to cheer them all up.

"Perhaps we could all go on an outing together," she suggested shyly at lunch one day. "Just us, without grown-ups."

They all thought it was a good idea and accepted that Crishell would be with them because it was hers. They spent ages discussing where to go and what to do.

"Ice-skating!" said Kester.

"A football match," said Raj.

"The zoo," said Maria.

Grace and Crishell talked about going to the movies – "Boring," said Raj – or having a picnic – "Too cold!" said Maria.

But when Grace talked to her mother that evening, it seemed as if there was nothing they would be allowed to do on their own.

"It's too risky, honey," said Ma.

"How can it be risky to go to the zoo?" asked Grace. "Do you think we'd climb in the lions' cage?"

"No, but you'd have to get there," said Ma. "And you're all still too young to travel on the bus or tube by yourselves."

"But when will I be old enough?" said Grace. "There are some kids in my class who come on the bus by themselves."

"That's different," said Vincent, who was having dinner with them. "It's a school bus, not a public one."

Grace wanted to say, "What's it got to do with you?" but she didn't want to be sent to her room, so she kept quiet.

But the next day, all of the friends had the same story to tell and all were indignant.

"We aren't allowed to do anything without having a grown-up around," grumbled Kester.

"It's so unfair," said Crishell. "My mother is always saying how she wants me to be more independent."

"And mine makes me do lots of jobs at home that grown-ups are supposed to do," said Maria, "like looking after the little kids."

"What do they think's going to happen to us if we go out on our own?" demanded Raj. "Do they think we're going to get kidnapped at the ice-rink or the footie?"

Russell was listening to their conversation.

"You don't have to do what they say, do you?" he remarked. "You could just bunk off school and go out on your own."

Normally they would never have listened to anything Russell said, but today, for some reason, it made them think. Up until now, they had all done more or less what their parents wanted. But this winter, with the changes it was bringing, was making them restless. They all felt old enough and responsible enough to have more freedom than they were being allowed.

None of them had ever bunked off school or forged a note from their parents before, but suddenly they were seriously considering it.

"But how can we?" whispered Maria. "We have rehearsals every day and Ms Woollacott would surely suspect something if five of the cast went missing at once."

"Not on Thursday," said Grace. "It's the waking-up scene and we're not in that."

They all looked at one another. It was true. It was the one day which wouldn't do the play any harm. And there were lots of children having days off with sore throats and coughs and colds, because the winter term was always like that.

Grace's heart was pounding at the thought of deceiving her nana, though she was pretty sure she could write a note that would look like her mother's handwriting.

The day of their adventure came. Because the weather had got so much colder, they had decided on skating in the park. The pond would be quite thickly-iced. So that they wouldn't have to take their skates to school, they smuggled them over to Grace's one by one during the week and hid them behind the bushes in her garden.

There would be a risky moment when they walked back to Grace's after Nana had dropped her at school, but Grace knew that her nana went and helped out at a community centre on Thursday mornings, so they thought it would work out.

And when Thursday came, there had been a heavy snowfall in the night, so everything looked perfect for their winter adventure. But Grace's courage nearly failed when she saw Nana waving her goodbye from the car. She dodged back outside the gate and hid behind a postbox. Soon the others joined her and they moved off quickly, not waiting for the school bell to ring.

Everyone was having second thoughts on the way back to Grace's, but when they got on the bus to the park it was different. They didn't go skating straight away, since they had the whole day to themselves. They climbed trees and went on the swings and the slide. It was great with hardly anyone else around, though there was a scary moment when the park-keeper asked why they weren't at school.

"Chickenpox," said Crishell quickly, and they were all so bundled up in hats and scarves that he couldn't tell they had no spots. The keeper hadn't had chickenpox himself, so he kept well away from them after that.

"Let's make a snowman," suggested Kester and they did, but it wasn't a very good one without a hat or scarf or a carrot for a nose. By the time they'd finished it, their gloves were all wet and they were shivering with cold, so they went to the kebab van near the gates where Crishell bought hot chocolate for everyone.

"Chickenpox," said Grace quickly, before the kebab man could finish asking why they weren't at school.

They took their drinks to one of the wooden tables in the park and ate their packed lunches, even though it was only half past eleven. Without her even asking, the other four all gave Crishell extra bits and pieces.

"We are having a picnic after all," said Maria.

"I wish we had a sledge," said Kester.

"I don't think we could have hidden that in Grace's garden," said Crishell.

"We could look for the North Pole here," said Raj.

And then they all had to explain to Crishell about the games they played in Grace's garden – and that made Grace feel peculiar again, because they wouldn't have had to explain anything to Aimee.

In the end, they decided to start skating because the snow was falling again and they didn't know how long they would be able to stay outdoors.

The pond was looking very beautiful, iced over between bare trees with the snow falling lightly on it, powdering the surface like icing sugar. There were benches all around it, where the children changed into their skates with stiff frozen fingers.

At first the skating was wonderful. They could all skate quite well and it felt so free to go flying across the ice without holding on to anyone or anything. But Grace had been feeling uncomfortable all day and the feeling was getting worse. The last time she had

come skating, last winter, Nana had been sitting on one of the benches in her parka, and Grace wished she were sitting there now.

There was someone sitting on a bench, eating a sandwich in spite of the wintry weather, but Grace couldn't see properly because there was snow on her eyelashes.

Suddenly she heard a loud C-RACK! and a splash and a shout. Someone had fallen in!

Grace skated cautiously towards the sounds.

"It's Crishell!" shouted Maria. "The ice gave way!"

Kester was crawling on his tummy across the ice towards the big black gash in the smooth surface where the ice had cracked. Raj was knotting his and Kester's scarves together. Grace could see what they were going to do.

In a flash, she spun on the spot and skated back to the bench on the bank. She could see now that the person eating lunch was a man. He was standing up and shading his eyes, peering towards the children.

"Help!" gasped Grace, breathless, forgetting all she had ever been told about not talking to strangers. "Someone's fallen in the water!"

The man immediately got out his mobile phone and called the emergency services. And then Grace got a shock almost worse than knowing Crishell was in the icy water. As soon as she heard the man's voice, she knew it was Vincent.

Grace tripped off the edge of the ice and hurled herself at him.

"Grace!" said Vince. "What on earth…? What's happened? Where's Nana? Why aren't you at school?"

Grace felt a hysterical giggle bubbling up in her throat and almost said, "Chickenpox." But instead she tugged at Vince's sleeve.

"Never mind about that now. It's my friend Crishell who's fallen in. Can't you do something!"

Vincent ran round the side of the pond to get nearer to Crishell. He stepped on to the ice, but as he got closer to the broken bit, slithering and stumbling as he went, there was another ominous crack.

"Oh stop!" cried Grace, "You're too heavy." She was crying now and the tears froze on her face.

Kester hadn't got to the water yet, but he had thrown the knotted scarves so that they almost reached.

Grace saw a dark head bob up in the water.

"It's no good," said Maria. "You're too heavy too, Kester. Let me try crawling."

"But you're not strong enough to pull her out," said Kester.

"You can hold my legs," said Maria, "and Raj can hold yours."

Grace was twirling around in an agony of indecision. She wanted to go and help her friends but now she was worried about Vincent, who looked stranded on the ice. What if he fell in too?

"Hold on, Crishell," she yelled. "The fire brigade are coming." Then she skated back to Vince, took his hand and slowly led him back off the ice to the bank.

Cautiously, Kester backed along the ice and Maria crept forward. She got much closer to the water and was able to throw the scarf to Crishell. She pulled, and Crishell moved closer to the ice. But she was too cold and wet to climb out, so Maria had to lean over and tie the sodden scarf around under her armpits. Then Maria tugged Crishell and Kester tugged Maria and Raj tugged Kester.

Grace wanted to get back on the ice and tug Raj, but Vincent refused to let her. He had her in a bear hug, which helped her stop shivering. But it didn't stop her crying. She buried her face in Vince's coat and it was from there that she heard the sirens wailing.

"The fire engine's coming!" she sobbed. "Thank goodness."

The firefighters got to the pond just as the children pulled Crishell free of the water. It was as well that there were ladders for the children to crawl across, because they were all exhausted, wet and freezing cold. An ambulance arrived too, and soon all five children were wrapped in silvery blankets and on their way to the hospital. Vincent came with them and phoned all their parents on the way.

They looked a sorry sight when they arrived in casualty. "What on earth..?" said the triage nurse when she saw them. Then, to Vincent, "How did they get into this state?"

"It wasn't his fault," said Grace. "He didn't even know we were on the ice. We bunked off school."

The nurse tut-tutted even more when she heard that, but soon the children were in cubicles, having their wet clothes stripped off and being wrapped in more insulated blankets.

Grace heard the nurse telling a doctor, "Some dad he is, letting his kid and her friends cut school and go skating."

Grace wanted to say, "He's not my dad," but, warm at last and completely exhausted, she couldn't get a word out and fell into a deep sleep.

Wicked Grace

The gang were in so much trouble. The only thing that stopped them being in even worse trouble was worrying over Crishell.

Nobody went to school next day. Crishell was kept in hospital overnight, "for observation", but the others were allowed home and told to take it easy. So no one got told off until Saturday morning, when all the gang and their parents met at Crishell's. By then Crishell herself was back home and lying on a sofa wrapped in a blanket, while everyone else sat round. It was pretty crowded with five children and eight parents.

Grace had more grown-ups there than anyone else because Vincent had come with Ma and Nana. "I expect I'll be three times as told off as Kester or Maria," thought Grace. She hadn't slept well since she woke from her cat-nap in Casualty. She kept having flashbacks of hearing the ice crack and seeing her friend's head bobbing in the black water.

No one seemed to know where to begin. Eventually, after lots of fussing round with coffee cups and introductions, Kester's mother said, "I think we should hear what all the children have to say about Thursday."

For some reason, everyone was looking at Grace. She felt very uncomfortable but she knew she had to get it over with.

"We were upset because our parents wouldn't let us do anything on our own, so we decided to cut school for the day," said Grace.

"And whose idea was that?" asked Raj's dad.

"It was Russell's really," said Crishell quickly.

"Who's Russell?" asked Maria's mum.

"He's just a kid in our class," said Maria.

"We don't have much to do with him," said Grace.

"And it wasn't his fault," said Kester. "He suggested it but we were the ones who did it."

"Carry on, Grace," said Ma.

"Well," said Grace. "We decided to go to the park and go skating. We had no idea the ice wasn't safe. And then Crishell fell in and

Kester and the others pulled her out. That's it really, except that we're all very, very sorry."

The rest of the gang murmured agreement.

"So Crishell just went along with you?" asked Crishell's mother.

"No, Mummy," Crishell cut in. "I already told you. I was as much in on the plan as anyone else. It was my idea in the first place for us to go out to cheer everyone up."

"Thank goodness Ava's friend Vincent was there with his phone," said Raj's mother. "Who knows what would have happened if the emergency services hadn't got there?"

"It seems to me," said Kester's mother, "that we need to talk about what we've all learned from this."

"And how they should be punished," said Raj's father.

"May I say something?" asked Vincent. "Speaking as someone who was there, I can assure you that these kids were all so scared that I don't think they'll ever do anything like this again. Am I right?"

Everyone nodded.

"So I think," continued Vince, "that they

have had their punishment already. What none of the rest of you saw was how brave they were. I couldn't help Crishell because I was too heavy for the ice and, although the emergency services got there very quickly, it might have been too late if the children hadn't already pulled her out. It was really her friends that saved her."

Vincent stopped. He wasn't used to making such long speeches. Grace was feeling very strange about how he had stuck up for them and she was secretly ashamed, too, because she hadn't helped pull Crishell to safety.

"But they took a terrible risk," said Maria's mother. "They might all have fallen in."

"I agree," said Nana. "But it shows what good hearts they have."

"The important thing," said Ma, "is that you must all realise why we said you were too young to go out on your own. The ice was unsafe. No one ever goes skating on that pond except when there is a grown-up on duty. I don't know what the park-keeper was thinking of, letting you on it."

Grace and her friends exchanged guilty glances.

"It wasn't his fault," said Grace. "He didn't see us." She didn't want the keeper to get into trouble because he was scared of their imaginary chickenpox.

"Are you going to tell Ms Woollacott?" asked Kester. It was the question they all wanted to ask. They had a horrible feeling that their punishment from school might be to give up their parts in the play, even if their parents didn't think they needed any more.

"Well," said Raj's mother. "We've already had to say something, to explain why you've had two days off school."

"I said Kester had got soaked to the skin and I was keeping him at home to make sure he didn't get a cold," said his mum.

It seemed as if everyone had said something similar.

"Do you think the school has to know?" asked Maria's mother.

"Definitely," said Nana. "These children did something wrong. They missed their lessons in order to have fun and the school needs to know that."

"But we can say," said Crishell's mother,

"that we have dealt with it at home – can't we?"

And the children were made to promise solemnly that they would not bunk off school again and not tell any more lies.

"I'm glad my dad's gone," whispered Kester. "He would have thumped me."

All in all, the gang thought they had been let off lightly. The only punishment they had at home was to be grounded until the end of term, which was only just over a week away. And after an anxious weekend, they found out that their only punishment at school was not to be allowed to sit together in class for what was left of term. Ms Woollacott was much too anxious about the play to make them miss that – especially since they had already been away for Friday's rehearsal.

Everyone was glad to throw themselves into the play again. For Grace particularly, who loved acting and stories, it was wonderful to escape into the world of magic. Her nightmares began to go away and, even though she wasn't allowed to sit with her, it made Grace feel good to know that Crishell was now a real friend. And they still got together at rehearsals.

The day of the performance came at last and the children were as nervous as when they acted in a real theatre, even though it was only in the school hall. The younger classes' performances came first – the little ones doing "The Night before Christmas" and "Rudolph the Red-Nosed Reindeer".

Then it was time for Grace's class. She peeped through the curtain and saw all the gang's parents sitting in the same row. Vincent was there between Ma and Nana, but somehow Grace didn't mind that now. She was sad, though, to think that Mrs Myerson wasn't there to see the play.

A boy called Robert stepped out in front of the curtain and spoke the prologue which Grace and Crishell had written:

Welcome to our school today,
We hope you like our Christmas play.
Our fairy tale is up to date
And we don't want to make you wait,
So now it is my pleasant duty
To introduce our "Waking Beauty".

Grace found herself mouthing the words. She looked over to Crishell and saw that she was doing the same.

The curtains drew back and Russell and Lynette were revealed in their cardboard crowns and home-made robes. "Oh, how I wish I had a little baby!" cried Lynnette dramatically – and the play was under weigh.

In no time at all it was the christening scene. The audience laughed heartily at the motley collection of christening guests. They specially loved Superman and Madonna. All the fairies and heroes had rhyming speeches which they declaimed with gusto.

And then it was the turn of the Wicked Fairy. Grace crept on stage menacingly, while all the other guests were pretending to drink champagne and have a good time. But some people in the audience spotted her and started to hiss. Grace turned her face, which was covered in green make-up, and snarled at them, which made them hiss all the more.

"Ha-ha!" cackled Grace. "Someone seems to be having a party and *someone* seems to have forgotten my invitation!"

The scene went swimmingly, with Grace pronouncing a very convincing curse on the princess, who was called "Slumberella" in this version. Then up popped Bonnie and changed the death-curse to the sleeping one and Grace snarled and hissed her way off stage in a terrible rage, to a huge round of applause.

The curtains swished closed and Robert came out with a placard saying "SIXTEEN YEARS LATER". A herald came on and read out a proclamation by the king, banning all needles, pins, brooches and any other sharp things from the kingdom.

Backstage, children were scrambling off and Natalie was coming on as Slumberella in a pink ballet dress. Grace was hiding behind a cardboard door, wrapped in a white lace tablecloth, with a real spinning-wheel, borrowed from the local library's artefact collection. She could see that Natalie was trembling, so she whispered "Good luck!" and Natalie smiled nervously and said, "Thanks – you too!" and the curtains swished open again.

Then Grace didn't feel nervous at all. She never did, once she was acting out a story.

She wasn't Grace any more, just a really wicked fairy pretending to be a kind old lady. Fleetingly, she thought about Mrs Myerson again, who really had been a kind old lady and not the witch that Kester once thought she might have been.

But then Slumberella touched the spindle and fell down in a most convincing swoon, and Grace threw off the table-cloth and pranced around the stage in triumph while king, queen and courtiers rushed on – only to fall asleep in dramatic mid-air poses.

When Julio kissed Natalie awake and she sprang to her feet and sang and danced to a Madonna record – although she was only miming – the audience erupted. All the heroes and fairies came back on stage for a grand finale and joined in the dancing – even Grace, who got a specially loud clap. "Encore, Grace!" someone shouted.

And at the end of the play, Ms Woollacott gave Grace and Crishell a box of chocolates each for writing the script and the class gave Ms Woollacott a bunch of flowers.

When Grace fell exhausted into bed

that night, her mother said, "You were wicked, Grace!"

"Oh, Ma," said Grace. "In future, I promise I'll only ever be wicked on stage!"

Grace Moves On

It was the Christmas holidays and Grace could be with her friends again. They were all a bit hyper since the play, except for Maria, who was more than usually quiet.

The day before Christmas Eve, when the gang were all round at Grace's, it had been snowing again and they made a proper snowman. It was very satisfying to give it one of Grace's Grandad's old hats and a scarf and pipe, as well as a proper carrot nose and real coat buttons from Nana's button box.

It looked so good when it was finished that Grace said, "We should get Crishell to come and see it. It's so much better than the one we made in the park."

The boys agreed, but when Grace turned to Maria, she saw that she was quietly crying. Grace was horrified. She had been here before.

"What's the matter?" she said. "Don't say

you're leaving too. Is your mother going to send you to that new school after all?"

Grace had a horrible feeling that, if this was so, it would be because of the escapade in the park.

She flung her arms round Maria. "No, you can't go. It wasn't your fault!"

Kester and Raj came and huddled round Maria too so that she had to struggle out of a heap of arms before she could speak.

"No, I'm not going to a new school," she said. "I'm not leaving. That's not what it is." And she wiped her eyes on the back of her wet glove.

"What is it, then?" asked Grace. "You must tell us".

It took a while, but eventually Maria said in a very small voice, "Is Crishell is going to be the fifth member of the gang?"

Grace and the boys looked at one another in silence. They had all had this idea, but no one had liked to mention it first.

"Would that be so terrible?" asked Grace.

"Don't you like her?" asked Kester.

"I didn't use to," said Raj. "But I do now.

She's different since we pulled her out of the pond."

Maria shook her head. "It's not that," she said. "I do like her, anyway. It's just that…when Aimee left, I thought perhaps I would be Grace's best friend. And now I think it will be Crishell and I still won't have a special friend of my own."

Poor Maria disappeared under a heap of friends again. Then they all went indoors and Nana made them hot chocolate – after she had admired the snowman.

While they drank the chocolate and dried their hats and gloves on the radiators, Grace thought about what had just happened. She remembered how jealous she had been of the new girl until Mrs Myerson had pointed out that it might be the other way round. Being jealous was one of the worst feelings she had ever had. She remembered having that feeling in the Gambia too when she saw Papa with his new wife and children. It was a feeling of being pushed out and not needed and she didn't want Maria to feel that way.

"Let's meet up as soon as we can after

Christmas," she said, "and we'll have a proper vote on whether to invite Crishell or anyone else. And if Maria doesn't want her, it won't happen."

But it still didn't seem enough, so when Maria's mum came for her, Grace whispered, "I am your special friend. Really, Maria."

And then it was Christmas Eve and the flat suddenly seemed much smaller than usual as Ma and Nana and Grace tried to wrap presents without each other seeing, stuff cloves into oranges for the mulled wine and into onions for the bread sauce, and put up Christmas decorations.

The weather turned mild. "No white Christmas for us," said Nana.

"No," said Grace. "Look! Our snowman's melted!"

But when she brought in the wet hat and scarf and other things, Ma was quite cross.

"Really Ma!" she said to Nana. "Are you still keeping all of Papa's old stuff? We just don't have room in this flat. And now it's all wet. Grace, take it out of the kitchen."

"No, child, give it here," said Nana.

And that was the first time Grace had ever heard her ma and Nana fall out. Nana put the scarf and hat in the washing machine on a cool wash with some of Grace's jumpers and no more was said. But there was a bit of an atmosphere for a few hours.

Vincent was coming to spend Christmas day with them and Grace thought maybe that was why her mother was extra jumpy. He was also going to take her and Grace and Nana out for a meal on Christmas Eve night, so they had to get all their jobs done early. Ma was still in the shower when the doorbell rang.

"Hey, Vince," said Grace when she let him in. "You do look silly."

"Why, thank you Grace," said Vince. He was wearing a Father Christmas bow tie that lit up when he pressed a switch, as he was doing now.

He sat down and chatted with Grace and Nana while Ma finished getting ready and he let Grace try on his tie, which was a clip-on one. Then they all went to a smart Chinese restaurant where Vincent had booked a table for four. Nana and Ma were all smiles again by the end of the evening.

When they got back home, Grace was yawning and Nana said, "Grace, girl, stop now. You've got me doing it too." And they both yawned and said they were going to bed.

"Goodnight, Vince," said Grace. "See you tomorrow."

"I'll be in to see you in a minute to say goodnight," said Ma. But Grace never knew if Ma did come in, because in a minute she was asleep.

In the morning, she climbed into Ma's bed to open her stocking and Nana brought them all a cup of tea and sat down beside them in her dressing-gown.

"What a squash!" she said. "Grace, you're getting too big for this."

But Grace thought she would never get too big for opening her stocking in Ma's bed. "You'll just have to get a bigger bed, Ma," she said.

"Well, I just might have to," said Ma.

Nana went to get dressed for church and Ma said, "Stay a minute, Grace. You know how that charter you made said that grown-ups should tell you things? Well, I've got something to tell you. It's not great timing, but you must blame Vince for that. You see, last night, after you and Nana had gone to bed, he asked me to marry him."

Grace's eyes grew so big, they took up most of her face.

"Aren't you going to say anything?" asked Ma.

"What did *you* say?" asked Grace.

"I said I would love to," said Ma, a bit shyly, "but I also said we had to wait and see if you would be OK with it."

Grace felt as if her heart was going to explode inside her pyjama top. She didn't really know if she was OK with it. She liked Vince now and she knew that Papa and Ma were never going to get back together. So she felt sad and excited at the same time.

"Where's the ring, then?" she said.

"Oh, Grace," said Nana, and they both had a hug and a little weep. When Nana came to chivvy them to get ready for church, she saw the ring in its velvet box and had to sit down and fan herself.

The rest of the day went in a whirl for Grace.

They were late for church and when they got back, Nana realised she'd forgotten to put the turkey in. So when Vincent arrived, they were laughing and pulling crackers. He saw straight away that Ma was wearing his ring.

"Oh, Ava," he said, and gave her a big kiss.

When Ma explained that lunch would be a little late, he said, "Then let's get on with opening our presents."

Grace's present from Vince looked very small, but when she opened it, it was a mobile phone. "Now you'll always be able to ring 999," said Ma.

"There's another number you can try first," said Vince, handing Grace a piece of paper.

"Whose is it?" asked Grace but Vince wouldn't say. It was another mobile number. Grace dialled it, not knowing who would answer. It rang for a long time. And then...

It was Aimee! The girls couldn't believe how sly their grown-ups had been, hatching this plot to give them both mobiles. Aimee hadn't opened hers and she had to tear off the wrapping paper while it was ringing.

Grace could hear Aimee's family laughing in the background and the sound of a cat yowling.

When the call was over, Ma said, "You and Aimee will have to learn how to send each other text messages or your phone bill will be enormous!"

"Can I ring Papa in Africa?" said Grace, just to see the look on her mother's face.

But when Papa did ring, later, Ma said, "Don't tell him about me and Vincent yet. I'll write to him about that."

They ate their roast turkey in the middle of the afternoon and it was the best Christmas dinner Grace could remember, perhaps because she was so hungry by the time they sat down to eat.

But the surprises were not over. When they had all settled down after lunch, Ma and Vincent on the sofa and Nana and Grace in the big armchairs, Nana said, "I have an announcement to make."

Everyone sat up straight. Nana never made speeches. Grace couldn't help herself. "You're not getting married too, are you Nana?" she said, then clapped her hands over her mouth in case she had gone too far.

"No, Grace," said Nana, "though I am thinking of a few changes. I don't have a nice boy like Vincent here to tempt me back into matrimony, but I do have something to tell you. I've known about it for a little while and I was waiting for the right moment. '

Grace was beginning to get worried. Ma looked surprised too, so obviously she didn't know what Nana was going to say.

"Gerda Myerson has left me her house," said Nana.

There was a long silence, while each of them thought about what this might mean.

"Now, I don't know where you plan to live after you are married," Nana said to Ma and Vincent, "But it seems to me that this little flat is pretty crowded already and, if Vincent doesn't mind a personal remark, he's not exactly the sort of person who won't take up much room, so…"

"No, no," said Grace. "You can't go and live in Mrs Myerson's house. You must stay with us. You've always lived with us. We can't change everything!"

Nana beckoned Grace over to sit on her lap. "There, there, honey," she said. "Don't get ahead of yourself. I'd just rattle around in Gerda's old house by myself. It's too big. What I wondered was whether you and your Ma and Vince would like to live in it. You could have a much bigger bedroom, Grace, big enough for Aimee to come and stay with you there. I could stay here and be just across the fence from you."

"But it's all dark and full of bars and bolts," said Grace.

"Nothing that a lick of paint and some new furniture and a crowbar can't change," said Nana.

"It's a very generous offer," said Vincent. "I was going to suggest selling my flat, anyway, but this needs thinking about."

"I don't know about you," said Ma, "But I've done enough thinking the last few days to last me a long time. Let's talk about it again tomorrow."

"And Grace," said Nana. "You can be involved in all the decisions. Just don't make up your mind too quickly! Now why don't we play Monopoly?"

So they spread the Monopoly set on the coffee table and played for hours. At the end, only Grace and Vincent were left, and then Vincent landed on Park Lane, which Grace owned along with a hotel. He dropped his head in his hands. "That cleans me out, Grace – you win."

—⚬⚬⚬—

The day after Boxing Day Kester, Raj and Maria came to Grace's flat. Grace had so much news to tell them that she was almost bursting with it. But there was something she had to say first.

"OK," she said, when they had told one another about their Christmas presents. "I suggest that we invite Crishell to be one of our gang. She can't replace Aimee, because no one can do that, any more than anyone can replace my papa or Mrs Myerson. But it was nice being five, wasn't it?"

Everyone agreed.

"And before we vote," said Grace, "I'd just

like to say that Crishell isn't going to be my best friend, whatever we decide. I'm not going to have a best friend any more. Now that Aimee isn't here, Maria is my oldest friend and Crishell can be my newest. Now, let's vote."

And four hands went up in the air.

MORE STORIES ABOUT GRACE
FROM FRANCES LINCOLN

BRAVO, GRACE!
Mary Hoffman

Grace's Ma is marrying Vincent and they're all moving next
door! Different friendships are emerging in Grace's gang too,
so when bullying and eating problems make an appearance
in class, Grace turns to Nana for advice. Then Christmas
brings an event which will change family life for ever...

STARRING GRACE
Mary Hoffman
Illustrated by Caroline Binch

It's the summer holidays and Grace and her friends are ready
for adventure. The circus is in town and the jungle next door
is just waiting to be explored. But then Nana falls and breaks
her ankle, and even worse, Ma gets a new boyfriend.
Grace feels as if her world is turning upside down!

AMAZING GRACE
Mary Hoffman
Illustrated by Caroline Binch

Grace loves to act out stories, so when there's a school
production of *Peter Pan*, she longs to be Peter. But her
classmates say that Peter was a boy, and besides, he wasn't
black... With the support of Mum and Nana, Grace soon
discovers that if you set your mind to it, you can do anything.

Frances Lincoln titles are available from all good bookshops.
You can also buy books and find out more about your favourite titles,
authors and illustrators on our website: www.franceslincoln.com